THE AMULET
OF AVANTIA

RASHOUK
THE
CAVE TROLL

With special thanks to James Noble

For Thomas Robert Maurice-Williams,
aka Tom-Tom

www.beastquest.co.uk

ORCHARD BOOKS
338 Euston Road, London NW1 3BH
Orchard Books Australia
Level 17/207 Kent St, Sydney, NSW 2000

A Paperback Original
First published in Great Britain in 2009

Beast Quest is a registered trademark of Working Partners Limited
Series created by Working Partners Limited, London

Text © Working Partners Limited 2009
Cover and inside illustrations by Steve Sims © Orchard Books 2009

A CIP catalogue record for this book is available
from the British Library.

ISBN 978 1 40830 378 8

7 9 10 8

Printed in the UK by CPI Bookmarque, Croydon, CR0 4TD

The paper and board used in this paperback are natural recyclable
products made from wood grown in sustainable forests. The
manufacturing processes conform to the environmental regulations of
the country of origin.

Orchard Books is a division of Hachette Children's Books,
an Hachette UK company.

www.hachette.co.uk

RASHOUK
THE
CAVE TROLL

BY ADAM BLADE

ORCHARD BOOKS

The Forbidden Land

THE DEAD VALLEY

THE DEAD JUNGLE

THE DARKWOOD

THE DEAD PEAKS

*A*ll hail, fellow followers of the Quest.

We have not met before, but like you, I have been watching Tom's adventures with a close eye. Do you know who I am? Have you heard of Taladon the Swift, Master of the Beasts? I have returned – just in time for my son, Tom, to save me from a fate worse than death. The evil wizard, Malvel, has stolen something precious from me, and until Tom is able to complete another Quest, I cannot be returned to full life. I must wait between worlds, neither human nor ghost. I am half the man I once was and only Tom can return me to my former glory.

Will Tom have the strength of heart to help his father? This new Quest would test even the most determined hero. And there may be a heavy price for my son to pay if he defeats six more Beasts…

All I can do is hope – that Tom is successful and that I will one day be returned to full strength. Will you put your power behind Tom and wish him well? I know I can count on my son – can I count on you, too? Not a moment can be wasted. As this latest Quest unfolds, much rides upon it.

We must all be brave.

Taladon

PROLOGUE

The cave was stuffy and airless, and the way ahead was blocked by a wall of stone. Fren tapped his cousin, Bly, on the shoulder. "It's a dead end," he said. "We should leave."

"We *must* find coal," Bly replied. "Winter will soon be upon us and I won't have my family going cold." He held his small, flaming torch aloft as he tapped at the wall with his pickaxe. "It's hollow," Bly smiled.

"We can smash our way through."

"We'd be crossing over to the Forbidden Land," said Fren fearfully.

Bly snorted. "I don't believe those stories about the Forbidden Land!" He slipped his torch into a crevice in the cave's wall. "Besides, there might be coal on the other side."

Bly hacked at the wall and Fren helped, despite his own fears. He and Bly swung their pickaxes with matching grunts that echoed off the cave walls like flung pebbles.

Within moments, they were on the other side.

Fren picked up Bly's torch and cast light over the new area. "Still no coal!" he growled.

Bly opened his mouth to reply, but his voice was drowned out by a fearsome thudding sound that made the ground vibrate beneath their feet.

"We should leave!" Fren shouted, as the thudding got louder. There was a familiar rhythm to it now.

Footsteps.

From out of the shadows came a creature more terrifying than anything Fren had ever laid eyes on. The Beast wasn't much taller than a man, but was five times as wide, and his shoulders scraped along the cave walls.

Fren recognised the creature, but only from old stories he had thought were fantasy. "A troll!" he cried, stumbling backwards as the Beast pounded towards them, his yellow teeth bared. Fren could see that the troll's hands were the size of large spades, and that the fingers on his right hand had long, jagged yellow nails. "Run!" he shouted to Bly.

But Bly did not move. "This wretched Beast won't stop me finding coal," he yelled back, raising his pickaxe.

The troll bore down on Bly, his heavy feet leaving deep craters in the ground with every step. By the light of the torch, Fren could see the Beast's large drooping ears and sunken eyes, pushed to the edges of his face by a wide nose that appeared to quiver as the Beast sniffed the air.

Bly gave a roar and charged straight at the hideous creature.

The Beast met him head on and swiped his right arm down, slashing at Bly with his sharp nails.

Fren screamed a warning but Bly made no sound at all – instead, he stood completely still. Fren gave a wail of fear and despair as he saw his cousin's skin darken to the colour of slate, and his body become stiff. Bly had been turned to stone!

With a sob, Fren fled back towards the mouth of the cave. Behind him, he could hear thudding footsteps and eager sniffing, telling him that the troll was close.

He heard a *whoosh* behind him as the Beast swiped down with his claws again.

Fren felt no pain as his body went still. There was only the cold, before everything went dark.

CHAPTER ONE

ESCAPING THE DEAD JUNGLE

"Almost there!" said Tom, as he swung his sword at the last section of wild undergrowth blocking their path out of the Forbidden Land's Dead Jungle.

"Great," said Elenna, as she led Tom's stallion, Storm, out onto the flat grassland. "I thought we'd never get out."

Storm whinnied in delight. Close behind, Elenna's pet wolf, Silver, yelped and ran around in wide circles.

Tom laughed and sheathed his sword. "I think they're happy they can stretch their legs again!"

"Although, to be fair, this place isn't exactly cheery," said Elenna, looking around at the dead grassland that stretched as far as the eye could see.

"I never knew that anywhere
in Avantia could look so dead
and depressing."

"Me neither," said Tom, thinking
of the beauty of the rest of the
kingdom and how the Dark Wizard,
Malvel, had tried more than once to
destroy it. It was because of Malvel
that Tom was on his current Quest.

The Dark Wizard had turned Tom's
father, Taladon, into a ghost, and
Tom had to find the six pieces of the
Amulet of Avantia to make his father
flesh and blood again. Malvel had
scattered the broken pieces of the
amulet around the kingdom's
Forbidden Land, where they were
guarded by six Ghost Beasts – evil
creatures who could switch from
real to ghostly form in an instant.

Tom had already defeated two of
them and retrieved two pieces of the
amulet. He vowed to overcome the
next four Beasts as well – though he
would have to do so without some of
the magical powers he possessed.

On a previous Beast Quest, he had
retrieved all six pieces of Avantia's
golden armour. Each piece had given
him a different power, although Tom

didn't need to be wearing the armour to use them.

But the armour did not belong to him. It belonged to his father. And now, every time Tom recovered a piece of the amulet, one of the armour's magical powers returned to Taladon.

Tom frowned as a feeling of disquiet spread through him. He had already lost the powers granted to him by the golden boots and the golden gauntlets. It appeared that he was losing his powers in the reverse order to which he had gained them. Therefore, if he succeeded in defeating the next Ghost Beast, Rashouk the cave troll, he would probably lose the power of the leg armour and no longer be able to run fast.

"Which way shall we ride?" asked Elenna, snapping Tom out of his thoughts.

"Map!" he commanded, stretching out a hand.

The air shimmered as a ghostly map appeared before his eyes. It was a gift from Aduro, the good wizard, to help them navigate the Forbidden Land.

Elenna joined him to study the map. "Look," she said, pointing at some mountains in the east called the Dead Peaks. "Didn't your father say we'd find Rashouk there?"

Tom nodded. He wondered how he would find fighting Rashouk now that he'd lost two of his powers.

"Are you all right?" asked Elenna, as the ghostly map evaporated. "You look worried."

"I'm fine," Tom insisted.

Elenna nimbly swung herself into Storm's saddle. Just ahead, Silver scratched at the ground impatiently. The clever wolf knew that they would soon be racing across the grassland at full speed.

"Do you want the reins?" Elenna asked.

Tom shook his head. "You ride. I'll run," he told her. "I should make use of the power of the leg armour while I still can."

Elenna clicked her tongue and Storm set off at a gallop. Silver ran alongside.

Tom took a deep breath and ran after his friends. Thanks to the magic he possessed, he caught up in moments. He was going to miss this power a lot – he loved the way he could look down at his own feet and barely see them because they were a fast-moving blur.

"I think Storm's tiring," Elenna called, after they'd covered a good distance.

"Let's give him a rest," said Tom, slowing down.

They came to a stop by a dense copse of trees. The branches were as black as coal and no leaves were growing on them. Silence hung heavily all around. As Elenna dismounted, Storm lowered his head to nibble at the grass. His nostrils flared and he pulled away immediately. The grass was coated in mould.

"Sorry, boy," said Tom, as his horse snorted in disgust. "Nothing for you to eat here. Not in this place."

Storm nuzzled Tom's neck. Elenna ruffled Silver's fur, making a bit more fuss of her pet wolf than usual.

She looked around. "Can anything actually *live* in a place like this?"

As if in answer, footsteps disrupted the silence like claps of thunder. Storm started, and Tom had to grasp his reins to keep the stallion from bolting.

Elenna jumped to her feet and ran to Tom's side. "It must be Rashouk!"

CHAPTER TWO

A MOMENT OF DOUBT

"If it is," said Tom, "for a cave troll, he's come very far out of his cave."

The footsteps grew louder and, looking ahead, Tom saw a large creature charging towards them out of the trees. It had shaggy brown fur and a long snout filled with misshapen yellow teeth.

"A bear!" Elenna gasped, and Silver

yelped furiously, showing his fangs.

Tom held tightly to the reins as
Storm tried to pull away. As the
creature got closer, he could see
the outline of its ribcage through the
thin, matted fur, and strings of saliva
dangling from its mouth. The bear
was ravenous and Tom and his
friends were its prey.

Tom gave Storm's reins to Elenna and drew his sword, preparing for battle. He could not let this creature come between him and his Quest.

"Stay back," he called to Elenna, as he stepped into the path of the bear. It may not have been one of Malvel's Beasts, but it was still twice as big as Tom, with cruel claws and jagged teeth that looked sharp enough to crunch through bone.

Tom's hand tightened round his sword as the bear got closer. His palm was uncomfortably sweaty. *The golden gauntlets made me a great swordsman*, he thought. *But I don't have them anymore!* He shook his head as if trying to empty it of his worries.

The bear was upon him now and it let out a deafening roar, blasting a jet of rancid breath that blew Tom's hair back.

What if I've become too reliant on magic? Sweat trickled into Tom's eyes and the sword hilt felt slippery in his grasp. *What if I'm not good enough when I'm just me?*

The bear raised its mighty clawed paws and Tom realised that his hesitation had cost him dearly – there was no time to defend himself!

A gust of air whistled past Tom's ear and he saw an arrow hit the bear's shoulder. The animal roared in pain, before stamping a path back to the cover of the trees.

Elenna appeared by Tom's side, her bow ready to fire another shot. But the bear had disappeared.

Tom dug his sword into the ground and leant on the hilt before taking a deep, calming breath.

"That bear was going to eat you alive," said Elenna, lowering her bow, "and you didn't even move!"

Tom turned, seeing her frown at him with concern. "I froze," he admitted. "I wasn't sure I could defeat the bear without my powers."

Elenna looked at him in amazement. "That's the silliest thing I've ever heard. You were brave long before you won those powers."

"I wish I could stop doubting myself," Tom said, turning away from her. "This is my most important Beast Quest… And I'm not sure I can do it!"

"TOM!" Elenna screamed from behind him.

He spun on his heel, sword raised. He had only one thought – *the bear was back*. A tree branch spun through the air aiming straight for his head. Tom raised his sword, and sliced through it. The two pieces fell to the ground.

Tom lowered his blade and looked over at Elenna, who was rubbing earth and bark from her hands.

"Did you throw that?" Tom asked in confusion.

His friend smiled and nodded. "You may have lost some of your powers," she said, "but that doesn't mean you're suddenly a bad swordsman."

Tom found himself smiling in return. "You're right," he said, sheathing his sword. "I can do this."

Elenna headed back to Storm and swung herself into the stallion's saddle. "No," she said, a twinkle in her eye. "*We* can do this."

Tom laughed as Elenna clicked her

tongue, getting Storm going again. Silver followed eagerly and Tom ran alongside them as they all headed around the copse of trees towards the Dead Peaks. Tom felt a swell of pride in his chest – Elenna was far more important to him than any power he could win or lose. He wouldn't trade her friendship for all the magic in Avantia.

But there was a big difference between a flying branch and an evil Beast. Tom knew big challenges awaited him.

"While there's blood in my veins," he muttered to himself, "I'll meet them and defeat the Beast!"

CHAPTER THREE

THE DEAD PEAKS

"I think we've arrived," said Elenna, bringing Storm to a halt as they came to a narrow path that led up to a mountain range.

Tom nodded as he took in the Dead Peaks, which were the colour of day-old ash. They were so tall, they disappeared among the dark clouds in the sky.

"It's too dangerous to ride Storm on

this narrow path," Elenna continued, dismounting.

"Yes, let's lead him up instead," said Tom. They started climbing the winding path. The higher they went, the narrower the path became, and they were forced to take the trail more slowly. The dark clouds hung low, and soon heavy rain began to pelt down, slowing them even further.

Tom frowned. "At the moment we're easy targets. We have no idea what could be around the next bend, and the path is so narrow it would be hard for us to retreat. Rashouk has the tactical advantage."

Elenna pushed her wet hair out of her face. "But there's nothing we can do about that. What choice do we have but to push on?"

Tom shook his head. "There is one

of us who can handle these paths at speed." He looked at Silver. "One of us can sniff out danger and warn the others."

Silver stepped forwards as if he knew Tom was talking about him.

Elenna ruffled the fur at the wolf's neck. "Go ahead, boy," she said.

Silver seemed to understand, as he darted forwards and disappeared round a tight bend in the path.

Tom looked back at Elenna. "We still have to tread carefully, for Storm's sake."

They made their way slowly, following the wolf's paw marks on the damp path. Silver howled excitedly up ahead. Tom felt his pulse quicken – it seemed like Silver was on the Beast's trail! The cave troll must be close.

"I hope we don't need to climb much higher," Elenna shouted over the driving rain. "Storm isn't happy."

Tom looked back and saw that the stallion was taking criss-crossed steps to stay on the road. His flanks were slick with sweat and his nostrils flared as he struggled to control his panic at the sound of thunder rumbling above them.

"All we know is that Rashouk lives somewhere on this mountain," Tom said. "Either Silver will find him, or we will find his lair – he's a cave troll after all, so his home must be a cave!"

Elenna nodded in agreement, her cheeks pinched with cold.

They turned a corner and came upon Silver, who was sniffing desperately at the earth. If there was a trail, it had gone cold. The path had widened out to a small plateau, but there was no sign of the Beast.

"What shall we do?" asked Elenna.

Tom squinted to see through the rain and mist that swirled around them. There was nothing but mountain rock and empty air. The rain chilled him to the bone and he could see that Elenna was shivering with cold.

Suddenly, up ahead, Tom saw something that made him smile with relief.

"There," he said, pointing at an outcrop not far up the path. "That should give us some shelter while we wait for the rain to stop."

Elenna gently urged Storm forwards again, and Tom and Silver followed.

Beneath the outcrop stood a mangy mountain goat. Tom knelt down and placed a hand on Silver's neck – he didn't want Elenna's wolf to startle the poor goat by running at it.

"He must be the only living thing up here," Elenna commented.

"Apart from the Beast," Tom replied grimly.

They scrambled under the outcrop.

It extended quite far out from the mountainside, but it wasn't very wide, so Tom and his friends huddled together.

Tom looked more closely at the goat. It was obviously scared, but not of them. Its eyes were wide as it glanced left and right. The goat was keeping a lookout for something.

The Beast?

"Elenna, do you think the goat has seen Rashouk?" Tom asked, still staring at the frightened animal.

Elenna didn't reply.

He turned round and saw only rain and mist. His friend was gone! *Had Rashouk got her?*

There was suddenly a loud sound, like rocks crashing to the ground. It came from further up the path, around the next bend.

"Elenna?" Tom yelled, running towards the sound. Up ahead, he could just about see what looked like a cave, which seemed to lead deep into the mountains. Beside its entrance, rocks were tumbling down. It was a landslide.

"Tom…I'm in the cave!" Elenna's voice echoed.

Tom could see now that Elenna was standing just inside the cave mouth.

He hurried towards her, dodging the avalanche of rocks.

"I had to take shelter because of the landslide," Elenna explained.

Tom took her arm. "We can't stay here," he said urgently. "Rashouk is a cave troll. This must be his home. That's why the goat has chosen to stay *outside* and get soaked rather than come in here."

As if in answer, a howling wind swept towards them, cutting through the sheet of rain outside. On the wind was a voice, now maddeningly familiar to Tom's ears. Malvel.

The Dark Wizard said only three words.

"Rashouk is coming."

CHAPTER FOUR

RASHOUK!

Elenna stared at Tom fearfully as
Malvel's voice died away.

"Look," he said reassuringly,
pointing out of the cave. "The
landslide has stopped. You'd better
get Storm and Silver. The Beast is
coming and we must be ready."

Elenna nodded and ran around the
bend, towards the outcrop.

Tom turned back to the cave.

Harnessing the magic of the golden helmet, which gave him super-sight, he looked deep into the cavern, right up to where the light from outside gave way to pure darkness.

The uneven walls were slimy and criss-crossed with moss-filled cracks and wide dents. Tom wondered if these dents were caused by the Beast's fist. Looking up, he could see ledges that jutted out of the rock face, hanging over the ground like the balconies at King Hugo's castle.

Tom's heart quickened. Perched on one ledge was a small, silver object with a patch of blue enamel at its edge, glinting in the faint light.

"The amulet piece!" he gasped.

"What are you waiting for?" Elenna's voice asked from behind him. Tom turned and saw her with

Storm and Silver. They joined him at the foot of the wall. "Go and get it!"

Tom hesitated. "What if it's a trap?"

"If it's a trap, we'll fight our way out," said Elenna, unhooking her bow and arrow. "Like we always do."

Tom nodded. "Keep watch for Rashouk," he said. "Warn me if you see anything strange in the shadows."

He turned back to the cave wall. If he'd still had the power of the golden boots, he could have jumped to the ledge in a single leap.

Tom clenched his fists determinedly. "Well, I'll just have to do it the old-fashioned way," he muttered and started climbing, slipping his fingers into the moss-filled cracks to pull himself up.

"Hurry, Tom," Elenna hissed, "before Rashouk comes back."

Tom pushed on. The cracks and crevices were getting more slippery and dangerous the higher he went. *Concentrate*, he told himself. *You're almost there.*

With one last heave, Tom pulled himself up onto the ledge, feeling a thrill of triumph. He had made it – the third piece of the amulet was in reach, and there was still no sign of Rashouk.

"Silver, be still," Elenna hissed at her wolf down below. Tom could hear Silver growling. He knew what that meant.

The Beast was near.

He grabbed the amulet piece, feeling a tingle of energy pulse through his hand. The other two pieces of amulet that hung from the leather strap around his neck almost seemed to vibrate. It was as though the first two fragments knew that another piece had been found. Tom shoved the third amulet section into a pocket in his jerkin.

All around him, the walls began to tremble and he could hear a thudding sound. *Thud, thud, thud.* Thin clouds of dust dropped from the roof.

Tom drew his sword and perched

on the ledge, looking down at his friends. He knew something large and terrible was coming and he got ready to protect them. Elenna, bow and arrow ready, walked in narrow circles, prepared for the Beast to attack from any direction. Silver walked in step with her, while Storm hovered nervously by the cave mouth.

Tom's eyes searched the cave. The thudding was getting louder. But there was still no sign of Rashouk.

Tom's eyes met Elenna's, and she looked up at him questioningly.

"I can't see him," he hissed. "I'm coming down."

Elenna's face froze in fear. She was looking past Tom now, at the cave's roof. "Behind you!" she cried.

Tom followed her gaze and felt his

heart stop for a moment. Rashouk the cave troll hung from two stubby stalactites as if they were vines, his wide, clawed feet dangling from short, muscular legs. He moved across the cave's roof like a monkey, from stalactite to stalactite. His grey eyes glimmered with evil delight as he came to a stop, hanging right above Elenna, who aimed her bow at him and shot upwards. However, as she did so, Rashouk took his ghostly form and the arrow passed right through him.

Tom desperately slid down the wall, stabbing his fingers into cracks to keep himself from falling, his forearms scraping against the rough rock. He could hear the Beast's low laughter echoing throughout the cave as the troll took his solid form once again.

The Beast then let go of the stalactites and dropped down on Elenna.

"Move!" Tom yelled, almost losing his grip.

Elenna dived out of the way, just as Rashouk fell to the ground. The troll landed so heavily that the entire mountain shook.

"No!" Tom exclaimed, as his hand slipped out of the crack to which he was clinging. He fell, desperately scrabbling for a handhold, but finding nothing.

"Tom!" he heard Elenna shout.

"Use the feather!"

He reached for his shield, which held the feather from Arcta the mountain giant that would protect him from dangerous falls, but it was all happening too quickly.

Crash!

Tom hit the ground. Fierce, hot pain shot up his leg. His right ankle felt like it had shattered into a thousand pieces.

Tom slapped his own face twice to stop himself from passing out. Elenna ran to his side, standing over him protectively and firing arrows at the Beast, while Silver stood by her ankles, growling at Rashouk.

But the cave troll didn't even bother to take his ghostly form, and simply batted the arrows aside. His grey eyes gleamed with dark joy as he drew himself up to his full height.

Tom got to his feet, putting all his weight on his uninjured leg. He drew his sword. Rashouk roared and charged towards him, sweeping Elenna and Silver aside with one massive arm. They were sent flying through the air, before hitting a wall and landing in a crumpled heap by the cave mouth, where Storm was standing. Tom roared with rage, but then felt a surge of relief as he registered the rise and fall of Elenna and Silver's chests. They were alive.

As Tom raised his sword to do battle with the Beast, Storm gave a high-pitched whinny, reared up on his back legs and galloped at Rashouk. The cave troll turned to meet him and leapt onto Storm's back, clasping his hands around the stallion's throat. Storm bucked wildly, trying to throw Rashouk off, his eyes rolling with fear.

Tom felt a sharp stab of panic as he noticed the Beast's massive, spade-like hands. Both ended in wicked-looking yellow claws, and those on his right hand were viciously long. They looked sharp enough to take off Storm's head.

The Beast was sniffing the frightened horse now, laughing wildly as he did so.

Tom hobbled forwards as fast as he could. How could he defeat this Beast while one of his legs was injured? But as Rashouk raised his right hand, ready to swipe at Storm with his deadly claws, Tom forgot his fears and doubts.

He dived towards the troll.

CHAPTER FIVE

BATTLING THE TROLL

Tom grabbed Rashouk's mighty arm at the wrist and, using his magical strength, dragged the Beast off Storm. As the stallion bolted towards the cave mouth, Tom gave a cry of pure rage and flung Rashouk at the wall. But the Beast turned his body and landed nimbly on his feet, like a cat.

Rashouk punched the ground,

sending fierce tremors through the floor, which made Tom's injured ankle feel even worse. Black spots danced in front of his eyes as the pain threatened to overwhelm him. Tom knew that he would have to find extra reserves of strength if he was to have any chance of completing this Quest.

"Watch out for Rashouk's claws, Tom," said Elenna, who had Silver by her side. She stood at the mouth of the cave, holding onto Storm's reins. Her voice was thin, as if she were in pain. Tom vowed to make the Beast pay for hurting her.

The cave troll swiped his right hand down. Just in time, Tom pulled back, and the sharp, jagged nails flew past his face in a yellow blur.

Rashouk was sniffing the air again.

Tom could see the thick, coarse hairs inside the Beast's nostrils quivering as he took in deep breaths. What was the troll sniffing for?

Rashouk took two lurching steps towards him. Tom sprang back and then to the left, changing his angle of attack. Rashouk's eyes still faced forwards briefly, before he once again sniffed the air and turned to face Tom.

He needs to smell me, Tom thought. *His sense of smell is stronger than his eyesight.*

Rashouk let out a loud roar that made the cave shake again. Tom stood his ground, trying to ignore the fiery pain in his ankle. The Beast stalked towards him. Tom backed up, but kept his sword high and his eyes locked with the Beast's.

He was determined to show no

fear. He would not give Rashouk the satisfaction.

"Tom!" he heard Elenna calling from behind him. "You're almost at the cave mouth. Be careful where you step!"

Tom felt no fear – only excitement. If the cave mouth was close, maybe he could somehow lure the Beast out onto the narrow path and over the mountain's edge. Not even a Beast could survive that fall.

"Follow me," he said to the troll. "I dare you!"

Tom took a step backwards and Rashouk followed. Tom bit his lip to stop himself from smiling. The Beast was going to fall for his trick.

"That's it," he said, taking two more steps back. "Come this way…"

Rashouk's face was tight with rage.

His yellow teeth were bared and his grey eyes narrowed.

Tom looked over his shoulder at Elenna, who stood by the cave mouth with Silver and Storm. The rain still pelted down behind them. "Be ready to get out of the way. I'm going to force the Beast off the mountain's edge," Tom said.

"You need to take just five more steps," she replied. "Be careful!"

"Don't worry about me," he said, turning to face Rashouk again. "If I fall, I can use my shield. This Beast won't be so lu—"

There was a flash of lightning, and for a single second, Rashouk's whole face lit up. His skin looked almost white in the fierce light. The Beast roared, covered his face with both hands and stumbled backwards.

"He doesn't like the light!" Elenna called out. "It hurts him!"

Hope flooded Tom's chest. The lightning may have interrupted his original plan, but he could use it to his advantage. He barely felt the pain in his damaged ankle as he charged at Rashouk, who was still blindly staggering backwards.

Tom dived at the troll, sliding along the rocky ground. As he passed through the Beast's legs, he swung his sword out. Rashouk's skin was thick and tough, and Tom had to use all his strength to make a deep cut.

The Beast bellowed in agony as thick, green blood seeped from the wound in his calf. With a snarl, Rashouk kicked out with his injured leg and sent Tom spinning through the air.

"Not again!" Tom vowed, unhooking his shield. The eagle feather embedded in it guided him safely to the ground.

Tom turned to fight the Beast once more but saw Rashouk fleeing back into the shadowy depths of the cave.

He started to hobble after the troll.

"Tom, help!"

It was Elenna.

Tom turned back towards the cave entrance. Elenna still had hold of Storm's reins, but the stallion bucked and spun in wild circles, dragging her with him. More flashes of lightning were cutting through the dark sky outside, followed by loud claps of thunder. The terrible noise was whipping the exhausted horse into a frenzy of fear.

Tom limped over as quickly as he could. "Easy," he said to Storm in a low voice. "You're safe now."

His voice seemed to do the trick. Storm stopped bucking, though he still walked in swift, ragged circles, his head thrashing from side to side. It made Tom's heart ache to see his loyal horse so confused and afraid.

He slowly reached out his hand and took a firm grip of Storm's reins, looping them around his wrist. "That's it," he said in a soothing voice. "Settle."

Storm began to calm down. The cave was almost silent now – not even Rashouk's footsteps could be heard. The Beast was either too far away, or he had found a place to nurse his wound before the next battle.

And there would certainly be a next battle.

And Tom would be ready.

The sky outside the cave was suddenly lit up by lightning again. It was immediately followed by a clap of thunder so deafeningly loud that it made Tom and Elenna jump.

Storm bolted.

Tom was swept off his feet as the stallion galloped towards the cave's entrance. Storm's reins were knotted round his wrists! He felt his head slam against a rock in the cave's wall and warm blood trickled down his neck. His body bounced and cracked against the cave's floor as he was dragged after the stallion. Tom tried to pull on the reins, but it was no good – Storm continued his mad flight. They emerged out onto the

narrow mountain path and headed
back towards the outcrop. Still Storm
wouldn't slow.

Beyond the path lay open space –
and they were hurtling towards it…

Towards their deaths.

CHAPTER SIX

THE MISSING PIECE

Using his remaining strength, Tom
reached up to put his free arm
around Storm's neck as he heaved
himself into the saddle. The darkened
skyline rushed towards him at great
speed. Any moment now, he and his
horse would tumble over the side
of the mountain and into that
endless drop.

Tom gripped the reins with both hands, pulling on them harder than he ever had before. Storm's head was wrenched back and his front hooves lifted high off the ground. With a second tug, Tom turned the stallion to the right, and his front hooves landed safely on the rocky mountain path.

Tom managed to free his hands from the reins and hugged Storm's neck. He could hear a quick, rhythmic pounding, and couldn't tell if it was the thumping of his own heart or Storm's.

"Good boy," Tom whispered, stroking the stallion's mane. "You did well."

He looked back at the cave and saw Elenna running towards them, followed by Silver.

"Are you hurt?" Elenna called.

"Nothing that can't be dealt with," said Tom, the pain in his ankle returning with a vengeance. He heard a bleating sound from further down the path. The mountain goat they had seen earlier trotted up and looked at them with a curious expression that made Tom laugh.

"What shall we do?" asked Elenna as Tom dismounted.

"We need to stay close to the mouth of the cave," he replied, sitting down. "You saw how Rashouk reacted to the lightning. He doesn't like the light, so we have an advantage if we stay here."

Tom felt his injured ankle. Even touching it created waves of pain that made him grit his teeth.

Elenna sat down beside him. "That Beast was horrible, Tom," she said. "The ugliest ever. I could practically *smell* the fear coming off Storm and Silver when they first saw him."

Tom's head shot up. *Smell…*

"That's it!" he said, remembering the way Rashouk sniffed at Storm's neck and laughed while he did so. "Rashouk smelled Storm's fear. That's how he tracks down his prey in the dark."

Elenna nodded. "That makes sense. Fear must have been coming off all of us. "

"Well, now we know, we can get close enough to defeat him. We'll not be afraid of Rashouk the next time we fight him."

Tom undid the jewelled belt he wore around his waist. He had earned the jewels on a previous Beast Quest, and one of them in particular was going to be of great use to him now.

"Is it broken?" Elenna asked, pointing at his damaged ankle.

"Not for much longer." Tom smiled grimly as he plucked the green jewel from the belt. It had the power to heal broken bones. He'd wanted to use the gem earlier, but he knew that it could take a little while to work, so he hadn't been able to do so during the battle. He placed the jewel against his ankle and concentrated. Ripples of energy left the gem and wrapped around the broken bones, knitting them back together. The magic was working.

"This Quest will be much easier on two legs," he said, putting the jewelled belt back around his waist. Standing up, he and Elenna guided Storm and Silver back to the mouth of the cave.

Elenna looked at Tom and pointed to his head, which had been cut open when he hit the wall as Storm bolted. "You should probably fix that. You need to be completely healed if you're going to take on Rashouk again."

"Right," said Tom. He took Epos the flame bird's talon from his shield and placed it against his temple. He felt the cut begin to close up. "I forgot I'd been knocked stupid a minute ago."

"How could you tell the difference?" Elenna joked.

Tom laughed and they gazed out beyond the mouth of the cave.

"The storm's fading," Elenna said after a moment. "We might not be able to use the lightning as a distraction."

"Then we'll just have to find another way to defeat the Beast. Won't we?"

Elenna smiled at him. "Of course! I'm glad we've finished half of our Quest and already have the amulet piece."

"Oh yes," Tom said, "I almost forgot."

"Are you *sure* your head's fixed?" Elenna teased.

Tom grinned and felt a thrill of excitement shoot through him as he reached for the amulet piece in his pocket. Elenna was right – they *were* halfway to completing this Quest.

He rummaged in his pocket and found...*nothing*. All he could feel was his own leg beneath his clothes.

Panic made his chest tighten. "It's gone!" he cried.

CHAPTER SEVEN

THE SMELL
OF FEAR

"It must have fallen out while you battled Rashouk," said Elenna despairingly. "We have to find it!"

"There's no time," Tom replied firmly. "The amulet piece is here somewhere – but right now, there's a Beast that needs to be defeated and we have to be ready."

Elenna's face clouded with concern.

"But...we don't have a plan."

"Let's think about what we know," Tom said, pacing around the cave. "We know that Rashouk prefers darkness to light."

Elenna nodded. "So we have to lure him out of the shadows and into the light – he'll be weaker then."

"Yes," Tom agreed. "We also know he can smell fear. That he loves the smell of it. Maybe we can use our own scent to lead him out of the cave?"

"Maybe," said Elenna, looking over at Storm and Silver, who stood quietly by the cave mouth. "But Storm and Silver have calmed down. So have we. We can't fake fear...can we? How can we make ourselves smell scared?"

Tom stopped pacing as he thought

hard. *How were they going to pull this off?*

Outside, the rain was easing up, and the clouds were clearing. Slivers of sunshine glimmered through the misty sky. It might not be lightning, but it was still light, and a potential weapon they could use.

But how to get the cave troll to leave his lair? Tom asked himself.

No solution came to him and reality began to intrude. He heard the howling wind that circled the mountains.

And the bleating of the mangy mountain goat.

That's it! Tom thought to himself.

Elenna grinned. "I know that look. It's your 'I've got an idea' look."

Tom smiled. "The goat," he said, walking out of the cave. "If we can somehow use his scent, we can trick Rashouk into coming all the way out here."

Tom looked down at the ground. For his plan to work they needed more than just the goat's scent; they needed something to disguise their own smell, so that it wouldn't dilute the goat's scent of fear. He heard Elenna follow him onto the path outside. Storm and Silver started to trail after them, but Tom turned and pointed at the ground. "Stay here," he said. "We're not going far."

Their four-legged companions seemed to understand. Storm stood proud and calm, while Silver lay on his belly – watching them closely.

"What are you looking for?" Elenna asked Tom.

"Something to cover our scent," he replied. "The goat's smell of fear has to be strong enough to lure Rashouk out of the cave and into the light, where he will be at his weakest. We can't afford to cover the goat's smell of fear with our own scent."

Elenna's nose crinkled in disgust. "I don't know about this."

"It's the only way," said Tom, scanning the ground again.

He heard Elenna's footsteps pause.

"Will this do?" she asked.

Tom looked up, just in time to see a handful of mud hit him squarely in the chest. Elenna was grinning at him.

Tom rubbed the mud into his clothes. "It's a start," he told her.

Soon, Tom and Elenna were not only throwing mud, but also crunching up some pungent-smelling leaves growing nearby and rubbing them all over their bodies.

"Let's hope this works," Tom said as they finished. He went to the goat, which was back beneath the outcrop. Tom approached as slowly and gently as he could. The goat didn't bolt. It simply kept its eyes on Tom with the same curious expression as before.

"I won't hurt you," said Tom,
as he got closer. "I promise."

As firmly as he could, Tom took
the goat by the flank and pulled
it towards the cave mouth. The
goat resisted, twisting its neck and

trying to nip at Tom.

Tom was surprised by how strong the goat was – but its struggles showed that the wiry animal was afraid. And, if it was afraid, then it was giving off a scent that would lure the cave troll from his lair.

"I hope this is enough to draw Rashouk out," said Tom. He kept a hand on the goat's neck. The animal had stopped struggling, but its eyes were still fearful.

Tom and Elenna stood side by side, facing the shadows. Storm and Silver waited just outside the cave. Tom hoped the scent of the goat's fear was curling through the air, deep into the cave, luring Rashouk from his hiding place.

He heard thudding footsteps. The sound startled both Storm and Silver, who inched further back. Tom glanced at Elenna, whose jaw was set in a determined line.

The cave troll was coming back.

"This time we're ready," Tom muttered, as Elenna reached for her bow and arrow.

It was time to defeat evil.

CHAPTER EIGHT

A NASTY SURPRISE

The footsteps stopped and started. Every time they paused, Tom could hear a frantic sniffing sound.

Rashouk was following his nose – all the way to the mouth of the cave.

"Come on," Tom whispered. "Come out to where we can fight you."

With a rasping roar, Rashouk tore through the shadows of the inner cave. Small rocks covered his bristly skin. The sharp fingernails of his right hand scraped along the walls, sending clouds of dust drifting through the air. Closer and closer he came, not seeming to care that he was headed towards the light outside.

Tom felt a quiver of excitement. His plan was working! Any second now, the cave troll would step into the light and be blinded.

"Get ready," he told Elenna.

But as Rashouk got closer to the cave mouth, he did not reel back in pain from the light. He just kept coming forwards. Tom's excitement was replaced by confusion. How could this be? He looked up. Dark, heavy clouds had filled the sky beyond the cave. Swirls of damp fog blocked out the golden light of the sun.

He turned back to Rashouk. The Beast's nostrils quivered and flared as he sniffed the air. His rheumy grey eyes shone with glee as he stalked forwards, swiping at the air with his razor-sharp claws.

Tom looked at Elenna hastily. "When I say 'now', jump out of the way."

The Beast raised his deadly claws.

"Now!" said Tom.

Elenna leapt to her right as Rashouk's clawed hand came down. Tom jumped to the left but tripped over the mountain goat, which was still standing beside him.

Rashouk raised his clawed hand again, his eyes fixed on the goat, who was paralysed with fear.

"No!" Tom cried. But he was too late. The Beast's arm came down, his cruel yellow nails cutting into the goat's right flank.

The goat did not utter a sound. Instead, its white coat appeared to darken and Tom heard a strange, crackling sound, like water freezing over. The goat now stood completely rigid, its eyes never leaving the cave troll. Tom didn't understand. The goat had survived the attack – why wasn't it running away?

Then he felt his stomach flip over as he saw the goat turn completely grey. He understood the crackling sound now. Rashouk had turned the innocent animal to stone.

Elenna's voice pulled his gaze from the goat. "Watch out, Tom!"

He looked at Rashouk and saw that the Beast's arm was raised once more. Tom just about managed to roll out of the way as the clawed hand came crashing down, the impact forceful enough to send three cracks shooting across the ground like lightning splitting the sky.

Rashouk gave a roar of a rage. He

had struck down so hard, his nails had got stuck in the rocky ground.

"The nails," Tom muttered to himself. "I have to chop them off."

He charged at the Beast with a furious cry, his sword held ready.

The cave troll ripped his hand free, throwing up earth and large jagged rocks that went flying in every direction. Some shards of stone bounced off Tom's body as he ran forwards, but he ignored them. Nothing would stop him from defeating this Beast.

Rashouk's claws, now free, slashed sideways, swinging so low that Tom had to throw himself to the ground to avoid being scratched. He had no intention of being turned to stone. But that wasn't the only thing he had to worry about – he had lured the

Beast right out of the cave, onto the mountain path, and either one of them could easily fall over the edge.

But it will not be me, Tom vowed.

"Get Storm and Silver away," he called to Elenna as he leapt to his feet.

Tom swung his sword to distract the cave troll as Elenna, dangerously close to the edge of the path, darted around the Beast, and lead the stallion and the wolf away from the cave and up a rocky incline to safety.

Tom stood facing Rashouk, keeping one eye on the troll's deadly nails. The Beast's fingers twitched and flexed as he sniffed the air. Tom couldn't understand Rashouk's thoughts like he could the good Beasts of Avantia, but he understood the troll's intentions. *He wants to turn me to stone right now.*

Tom stood, his shield raised. "Try it," he said. "I dare you."

But it wasn't the Beast's right arm that moved. It was his left – and Tom gasped as his sword and shield were knocked right out of his hands, and clattered to the ground.

There was no time to reach them.
Rashouk's right arm swung down
and Tom dived towards the Beast,
ducking beneath his clawed fist to
land in a ball at the troll's feet.

Tom jumped up and wrapped his
arms around Rashouk's wrist,
twisting hard. Immediately, the Beast
tried to shake Tom off. Rashouk then
lifted his arm and slammed it against
the side of the mountain, crushing
Tom. Dust and pebbles rained down
on both of them, making Tom's
eyes water.

But he did not let go. The Beast's
arm was as thick as a small tree, and
Tom had to use all his strength to
keep his fingers locked together as
the cave troll tried to dislodge him.

Roaring in frustration, Rashouk
swung his arm left and right, down

and up. As Tom's feet left the ground, he was briefly raised so high that he was sure he could see the whole of Avantia.

The dark sky and the distant scenery blurred and slid past him as Rashouk swung around. Tom let go of the troll's arm and somersaulted through the air to land on a ledge that jutted out of the mountainside, above the Beast's head. From this position, Tom slammed his fist into Rashouk's skull, leaving shallow dents. *I may not have my sword*, Tom thought, *but I still have the strength of the golden breastplate*.

"Go on, Tom!" cried Elenna, from the incline higher up the mountain. Silver and Storm howled and neighed encouragement.

Rashouk staggered back from Tom's

forceful blows and then reached up
to swipe him off the ledge. As the
yellow nails came hurtling towards
Tom, he slammed his fist into the
Beast's thumbnail – and it came off
completely. Tom saw spurts of green
blood shooting in all directions from
the ruined stump.

Rashouk howled and reeled away in pain while Tom dropped down from the ledge and landed neatly by his fallen sword and shield. One of the deadly nails had been taken care of, but there were still four others.

He scooped up his weapons and turned to face the Beast once more. He was going to finish this Quest right now.

"For my father!" he cried, racing forwards and swinging his sword up at Rashouk's wounded right hand.

But his blade did not connect with the deadly nails. Instead, it seemed to pass straight through the Beast.

Rashouk had taken on his ghostly form, Tom realised. The Beast began to laugh and Tom turned to face him again. The troll was still monstrous in size, but Tom could now see right

through him. He saw the outline
of the mountains and the statue that
had once been a live mountain goat.
Tom gazed at the Beast, who looked
triumphant.

This Quest was far from over.

CHAPTER NINE

WRESTLING A GHOST

Rashouk squatted on the ground and Tom knew the Beast was preparing to charge at him.

Elenna was descending from the incline.

"No!" Tom called. "Stay with Storm and Silver."

Elenna stopped halfway down. "But you need my help!"

"If Storm bolts again, he'll go right over the edge. We can't let that happen."

With a wild roar, Rashouk barrelled along the ground at great speed. Tom held up his sword and shield, even though he knew both would be useless against a ghost.

Thunk!

It felt like a stone wall had slammed into Tom, and he was sent tumbling back along the mountain path. Rashouk had shifted into his solid form at the last moment.

Tom got to his feet, tightening his grip on his sword. He saw that Rashouk was once more back in his ghostly form. The Beast seemed furious that Tom was showing no fear. With a roar, the troll charged again. Tom lunged to meet him, slashing at the Beast's claws.

Tom felt nothing but a rush of cold as he passed straight through the Beast. Then there was a powerful hand on his back. Rashouk – flesh and blood once more – pushed him forwards like an arrow from a bow, towards the edge of the mountain path and over the side.

Tom was dimly aware of Elenna screaming as he felt his body plummet downwards. With a yell of determination, he stabbed his sword into the mountain rock, burying the blade almost to the hilt. He hung there for a moment, catching his breath as his legs dangled above low-hanging clouds that obscured the ground below.

Relief washed over him. He had survived, and could afford to smile.

But he would need to come up with
a different method of attack if he was
going to defeat this Beast.

Tom freed one hand from his sword
and swung up to grab at the edge of
the mountain path. Yanking the
blade out of the rock, he scrambled
back up to safety.

Rashouk had his back to Tom. The troll was advancing towards Elenna, who still stood on the incline, bow and arrow raised. Elenna began firing arrows, but it was useless as Rashouk had returned to his ghostly form. Tom was certain that the cave troll would soon become solid – and there was no telling what damage he would do to Elenna and his other friends.

Tom stepped towards Rashouk as lightly as he could, hoping the Beast's hearing was as bad as his eyesight. The troll's transparent hide began to shimmer. He was becoming real again. This was Tom's chance!

But Rashouk was ready for him. He spun on his giant heel and swept his arm across the ground, flipping Tom into the air.

Time slowed down as Tom's body spun and turned. Down below, he could see that Rashouk was readying his deadly hand to scratch him and turn him to stone.

Tom had to strike first.

As he fell, he readied his sword. When Rashouk's hand came upwards, Tom brought the side of his blade hacking down, slicing off two more of Rashouk's deadly nails. Only the nail on his smallest finger remained intact.

The Beast roared in agony. Elenna loosed three quick arrows at Rashouk, while Tom landed neatly on his feet.

Well done, Elenna, Tom thought. *The Beast is so mad with pain and anger he doesn't know who to attack first. He's not thinking about changing back into ghostly form now. We've almost won!*

Rashouk turned to face Elenna. At the same moment, Tom dropped his sword and shield and sprang forwards, grabbing the troll's hand.

Using every ounce of his strength, Tom wrenched the Beast's arm back and forced the troll to scratch himself with his own jagged yellow nail.

Rashouk screamed as the nail made contact, tearing his grey hide. Thick green blood oozed from the wound. Immediately, the Beast fell still and silent. Tom heard a loud crackling sound that bounced off the mountain walls. Rashouk's whole body stiffened as his hide became a darker shade of grey.

The Beast was turning to stone. His own evil magic had been used against him. The transformation started at his head, bleeding all the way down his neck, his chest, his shoulders, his arms…

His arms!

Tom released his grip on the Beast's wrist just as it hardened to rock. Rashouk still loomed monstrously over him – but he was just a statue.

The third Ghost Beast had been defeated.

CHAPTER TEN

THE NEXT QUEST

"Well done, Tom!"

Elenna came down the slope and ran over to him. Storm trotted by her side and Silver circled Tom's ankles, yelping happily.

"See," she said, "I was right! It doesn't matter that you've lost some of your special powers. You're still the bravest person I know."

Tom picked up his sword and

shield. He sheathed the blade. It felt good to put it away for a while.

"I have three brave friends," he said. "I just follow their lead."

Silver howled happily as if in agreement. Tom patted his head. "Glad you're all right, boy," he said. He turned to pet Storm, but saw that his stallion's eyes were fixed on something beyond Tom's shoulder.

The statue of the Beast.

"It's over now, Storm," Tom whispered. "We're all safe."

But Storm reared up and bolted, before either Tom or Elenna could reach out and stop him.

Hooves clattering on the hard ground, Storm pounded towards the statue of Rashouk, not slowing for a second. He skidded to a halt and fiercely kicked the stone cave troll, sending it toppling to the ground.

Tom laughed as Storm cantered back to join them.

"That'll teach Rashouk to mess with us!" Elenna laughed.

Tom stroked Storm's flank. "Well done!" he said.

"Should we leave the Beast here?" asked Elenna.

Tom looked closely at the troll's face, frozen in an expression of rage. "No," he told her. "There's always a chance Malvel could reawaken Rashouk. We can't take the risk."

Elenna cautiously touched the stone troll. "What should we do?"

Tom looked beyond the statue, to the empty sky that stretched up from the mountain. "Maybe the Beast should take a little trip…"

Using the power of his golden

breastplate, Tom rolled Rashouk along the ground as easily as if he were an empty barrel. Elenna helped, and soon they had the Beast on the edge of the mountainside.

"Push!" Tom shouted, and they did.

Tom and Elenna cheered as they watched the statue of Rashouk fall, plunging through the thick clouds and quickly disappearing from sight. They heard the crash and splinter of stone as the statue smashed into the ground below.

Tom suddenly heard the sound of bleating. He looked over to where the mountain goat stood. He was no longer frozen – in fact, he was trotting along the mountain path as if he owned it.

Tom turned to Elenna. "Everything is as it should be."

"Don't get too happy," his friend warned. "We still have to find the missing piece of the amulet."

"Of course," Tom said. "Let's start in the cave."

Enthusiastic yelping cut him off. He and Elenna turned to see Silver emerge from the cave, a shining piece of metal in his mouth. The excited wolf raced over to them.

"The amulet piece!" cried Tom.

"I didn't even see Silver go inside!" said Elenna, laughing and ruffling the wolf's fur, as Tom took the fragment from his mouth.

"I don't think he needs us to give him instructions anymore," said Tom. He attached the new piece to the two fragments already on the leather thong around his neck. The amulet was half complete now. The shining blue enamel in the centre looked more impressive, and the odd lines and grooves etched on the back of the amulet pieces somehow looked more detailed and connected. For the first time, Tom could make out what they were.

"Roads," he breathed. "It's a map!"

Elenna joined him and looked at the etchings. She frowned. "Doesn't look like anywhere in Avantia, though," she said.

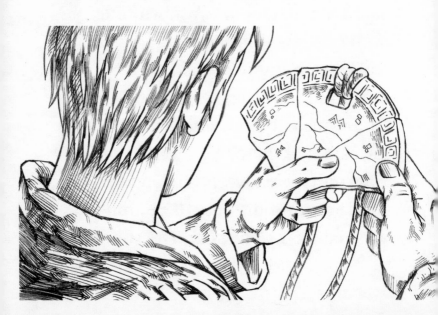

"Maybe it's not Avantia," Tom replied. "Maybe there are more secrets to this amulet than either Aduro or my father have told us."

"Another Quest completed."

Tom and Elenna both jumped at the sound of a familiar voice beside them. Tom's father had appeared in his ghostly form.

"Thank you," Taladon said, with a slight bow. Tom felt his heart leap as he saw the proud smile on his father's face. "You have restored another part of my strength. I am closer to being real again."

Tom squared his shoulders. "I promised I would not fail you," he said.

"And you are keeping your word," Taladon replied. "I could not have wished for a nobler son."

"Father," said Tom, holding up the half-complete amulet. "The backs of the fragments...do they show a map?"

Taladon sighed. "I'm afraid the secrets of the amulet are not mine to reveal," he said.

Tom almost pushed the point, but bit his tongue. The secrets could wait. For now, the most important thing was bringing back Avantia's great hero.

"You must head to the Dark Wood," said Taladon. "You no longer have the power to run incredibly fast, but you must still make haste. There lies your next challenge. The swift and cunning moon wolf named Luna."

Tom felt his face harden. "I don't care what Malvel puts in my path," he said. "I'll defeat all of his Beasts!"

"The very words I hoped to hear,"

said Taladon, nodding in approval.
"I must depart – but stay brave,
and stay loyal to each other. You
will prevail."

With a shimmer, Taladon's ghostly
form evaporated. The sun had come
out and was chasing away the rain
clouds.

"Of course we'll prevail!" said
Elenna.

Tom smiled at her as he reached out to grasp Storm's reins. "Come on," he said. "I can't wait to get off this mountain!"

The two friends walked Storm slowly back down the winding path, Silver racing ahead. Tom felt tired after his battle with Rashouk, but elated that his Beast Quest was half finished.

Malvel was still wreaking evil across the kingdom. And while that remained true, Tom would never give up fighting.

There were many more adventures waiting for him. And Tom was ready.

Win an exclusive
Beast Quest T-shirt and goody bag!

In every Beast Quest book the Beast Quest logo is hidden
in one of the pictures. Find the logos in books 19 to 24
and make a note of which pages they appear on.
Send the six page numbers in to us.
Each month we will draw one winner to receive
a Beast Quest T-shirt and goody bag.

Send your entry on a postcard listing
the title of this book and the winning
page number to:

THE BEAST QUEST COMPETITION:
THE AMULET OF AVANTIA
Orchard Books
338 Euston Road, London NW1 3BH
Australian readers should email:
childrens.books@hachette.com.au

New Zealand readers should write to:
Beast Quest Competition
4 Whetu Place, Mairangi Bay, Auckland, NZ
or email: childrensbooks@hachette.co.nz

Only one entry per child.
Final draw: 31 May 2010

You can also enter this competition
via the Beast Quest website: www.beastquest.co.uk

Fight the Beasts,
Fear the Magic

www.beastquest.co.uk

Have you checked out the all-new Beast Quest website?
It's the place to go for games, downloads, activities,
sneak previews and lots of fun!

You can read all about your favourite Beast Quest
monsters, download free screensavers and desktop
wallpapers for your computer, and send
beastly e-cards to your friends.

Sign up to the newsletter at www.beastquest.co.uk
to receive exclusive extra content and the opportunity
to enter special members-only competitions. It's the best
place to go for up-to-date info on all the Beast Quest
books, including the next exciting series,
which features six brand new Beasts.

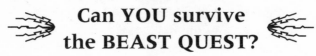

Can YOU survive
the BEAST QUEST?

Read all of Tom's incredible adventures as he battles
the fearsome Beasts sent by evil Wizard Malvel.
Together with his loyal friend Elenna, his trusty
steed Storm and Silver the grey wolf, Tom risks
everything in his fight for the freedom of Avantia.

Will good conquer evil? Or will Malvel and his
Beasts destroy the kingdom? As long as there is
blood in his veins, Tom is determined to stop him…

Do BATTLE with
your friends!

Each exciting story comes with FREE collector cards!
Cut them out and play with your friends. Keep an
eye out for a special exclusive collector card – check
the Beast Quest website for details.

www.beastquest.co.uk

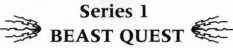

Series 1
BEAST QUEST

An evil wizard has enchanted the Beasts that guard
Avantia. Is Tom the hero who can free them?

978 1 84616 483 5

978 1 84616 482 8

978 1 84616 484 2

978 1 84616 486 6

978 1 84616 485 9

978 1 84616 487 3

978 1 84616 951 9

Can Tom save the baby
dragons from Malvel's
evil plans?

Series 2
 THE GOLDEN ARMOUR

Tom must find the pieces of the magical golden armour.
But they are guarded by six terrifying Beasts!

978 1 84616 988 5

978 1 84616 989 2

978 1 84616 990 8

978 1 84616 991 5

978 1 84616 992 2

978 1 84616 993 9

SPECIAL BUMPER EDITION!

Will Tom find Spiros
in time to save his
aunt and uncle?

978 1 84616 994 6

Series 3
 THE DARK REALM

To rescue the good Beasts, Tom must brave the
terrifying Dark Realm and six terrible new Beasts...

978 1 84616 997 7

978 1 84616 998 4

978 1 40830 000 8

978 1 40830 001 5

978 1 40830 002 2

978 1 40830 003 9

978 1 40830 382 5

Arax has stolen
Aduro's soul – and
now he wants Tom's...

Series 4
THE AMULET OF AVANTIA

Tom's Quest to collect the pieces of amulet from the deadly Ghost Beasts is the only way to save his father...

978 1 40830 376 4   978 1 40830 377 1   978 1 40830 378 8

978 1 40830 379 5   978 1 40830 381 8   978 1 40830 380 1